HERE

IN

THE

(MIDDLE)

OF

NOWHERE

also by

Anastacia-Reneé

Side Notes from the Archivist

AMISTAD
An Imprint of HarperCollins*Publishers*

HERE

IN

THE

(MIDDLE)

OF

NOWHERE

Anastacia-Reneé

Poems "Apocalypse 400," "Copycat Universe," and "Universe" were previously published in *The Future of Black: Afrofuturism, Black Comics and Superhero Poetry*; "Wearing a Cape," was previously published in *Ms.* magazine; excerpts from *26* were previously published by Dancing Girl Press; excerpts from *Answer (Me)* were previously published by Winged City Press.

HarperCollins books may be purchased for educational, business, or sales promotional use. For information, please email the Special Markets Department at SPsales@harpercollins.com.

FIRST EDITION

Designed by Janet Evans-Scanlon

Illustrations on pages iii, 3, 79, and 103 © VVadi4kastock.adobe.com
Tree illustration on page 1 courtesy of Barbara Tolbert

Library of Congress Cataloging-in-Publication Data has been applied for.

ISBN 978-0-06-322167-3

24 25 26 27 28 LBC 5 4 3 2 1

family tree

lucile (7)

lucile (6)

*

*

*

lucile (4)

bloody mary (3), prospect women

essie, laverne jay, luther aka bogeyman

lucile (5)

essie, townspeople,

forfuctioners

lucile (3)

the 33rd underground

laverne, hyacinth, jocelyn, harper & faye

bloody mary (2), luther sr. toast,

octavia: the wormhole between

motherboard space shuttle ship

granny

baby lucile (6)

lucile (2)

essie, landis

fore functioners

the atlantic apartment & residents

lucile(1)

lucy's sanctuary

cyclops women

luther, toaster oven mama

glenda the good witch, black girl vampire lisas

bloody mary (1)

grace, mailman, the devil, religious, leper

---

lucile (god) (mother)

parallel universe   current universe   alternate universe   glitch   prefuturo

Layer I.

in the beginning: lucile was god

(we) the ones made of nebula & who have traveled from far, far, far away from (here) worked on the space shuttle ship to the best of our natural ability, but lucile still had a slow yellow limp & systemic pain lodged in her motherboard. we do want to leave this planet, but we don't need to leave (right now). the repairs, on the one hand, seem minimal, but, on the other hand, seem as if—it could take—light-years. it is hard to say in the state (we are in). she has asked us, our space shuttle ship, to go on without her. as in let her rest. let her sit. cover her & keep going. of course we don't like the idea of her being tied (to this earth) |especially| with her ankles bound to soil |especially| with the tree like branches on her back. our space shuttle ship is an irrepressible one. & (we) the ones who traveled from far, far, far away from (here) will always be thankful. we were told to leave our 3rd eyes in our space shuttle ship in their cases with their own mothers. the mothers of the 3rd eyes see (it all) & they have told us not to sleep. for this reason we have been asked to avoid most things entertaining & to plant our dear lucile of the cosmos & nebula & stars & the infinity of magic (here).

~~visitors~~ you

come on.   come in.

stay.   awhile.

i pour sun tea in a mason jar with uneven chunks of ice & put the tip of my tongue on the barrel of the straw & sip it slow like an invocation to myself. i like to run my piano fingers against these turquoise louvered shutters slow so i can feel what they are communicating to me. could be telling me secrets. could be making plans. could be letting in the light. could be sounding off a warning. could be just a turquoise shutter.

i like to sit like a right angle   90 degrees & slightly slouched here with a piece of my dress under my butt & the rest of it hugging the tops of my knees, fanning my fan every which way & staring right here at my tree. i like to be barefoot with my legs wide as the milky way & my sweaty hips sunk deep enough to leave an imprint of myself & the black blades of my shoulders pushed into the cushion's floral design like grass & then i rest every eye for a spell. but as soon   i mean as soon as i do that   bees come buzzing & bumbling around me & i have to flap the pockets of my dress & baby i jingle   just a little bit because i always keep change somewhere deep in the crevices on each side. 5 pennies, 9 dimes & a shiny 2-dollar sterling-silver piece.   i sit. & sit. & sit some more (here) on this porch watching over my tree. all. the. time.

i am   lucile.

     i. am. mother
     of all luciles
     of all of you
     god.
     in this place
     in the middle of nowhere

you want to know if i am a star (here)?

     yes. a luminous one.

you want to know how many luciles
are mine?

      6

you want to know many times have they
each been around the sun?

―――

you want to know if you can see them?

     yes.

resurrection—
the act of rising
from the dead &
returning to life.

oh luciles   suga cubes
i know what it feels like
to be severed from your genesis
like a light-year
trapped to retroflect
the gurgling consciousness
of memory stained by
prepositional amnesia
you want to know
at what cost
which floods have you been in
what are you made of
& where are you traveling to
but   my daughters
lucile's maternal lineage
lucile's spirit
lucile's imprints
lucile's 4-dimpled smile
lucile's subplanetary alignment
first earth & cosmos
(here) is where every
lucile is.

to conjure
to be conjured with

a glossary of beings
in the town
to be a branch
or a parish   or a cemetery
or the wind   or a mother   or a spaceship
or a dream   or an alternate reality

                                        the luciles & the townspeople
                                    fling themselves against my trunk

you want to know if you ~~visitors~~ can see them

    yes. (here) at my tree

rib cages & hip bones
thickets of hair & shoelaces
tachycardia & phantom limbs
bridesmaids, eggshells, & hysterectomies
kisses (all kinds)
sometimes blowing kisses at me
at the ground   @ friends
disappearing selfies at my tree
afropod selves & aversions of selves
splintering selves & centering selves
i don't head-count but if i did i'd say
maybe a quarter till infinity
& still coming
i love black, shimmering holograms
projected on my bark
concentric ridges of dna
all. around.

i tell them through found objects
& sudden wind gusts
to keep it pushing
because sometimes life is both
flecks of horror & delight

           but
some of them are hardheaded
& don't want to hear
some of them can't help it
because they suffer with
the nausea of imposter syndrome
& migraines of spiritual impediments
crucifixes passed down
to ward off themselves
their telepathy
their knowing
their dreaming
their _____
a hurricane of lost languages
spinning tongues like inclement weather

some sigh
some scream
some sing
some spit
some slay _____
at my root

monsters   vampires   mortals   mermaids
citizens   priestesses   griots   witches
babies   animals   lovers   bloody marys
time-jumpers creatures   ~~visitors~~ you   _____

house—
relating to the place
where one lives.

lakay   crib   bungalow   shanty box ile
shotgun   quarters   apartment

dwelling   saltbox   residence   nest
house mother   house father
home—
(of an animal)
return by instinct to its
territory after leaving it.

you want to know if there is time jumping
& multiple versions of townspeople

  yes.

you want to know if you ~~visitors~~ you go inside (here)

  yes. if you plan to stay.

you want to know if you'll be visible to everyone in the town?

  no.

  & once i say you ~~visitors~~ may enter,
  you will no longer be just a ~~visitor~~ (here)

listen:

1. crooked metropolitan roads, plasma-colored dirt roads, marble roads, suburban pavement, & volcanic soil here in this place do not converge easy-peasy. it's everything. it's nothing. townspeople pretzel their bodies & bingo horror stories with the dead while they throw salt & shade. say things like: but is your vampire-bartender better at spades than my friend who gets her hair braided at the coven salon in lucile #3's parish? or: can i put my second soul on layaway & get a neighborhood discount for the way this human body fades to a morphine drip. there are roads which do not middle, only begin & end.

2. hidden back roads gravel holy in syncretism & plush lawns & citizens trip over the smallest of things & they know good & well the world above is a bigger dress to hem & there are things no one body can decipher. there are french-braided subdivisions & cornrowed patterns & wide city blocks of lavender, lime-green, & peach shotgun houses which appear closer in rearview mirrors. each one with its own labyrinth & lucile's skeleton key. this is a multidimensional place, inside a town, inside a city, inside a state.

3. humans suck on grudges like peppermint candy. when will they learn? no one wants a bloated stomach of floating regrets & red pepper flakes. no one wants to repetitively stitch up joys niggling tear. there are townspeople who try to close read each other as jigsaw puzzles. it doesn't work. like skating on sand like sopping up gravy with your right hand drenched instead of using a biscuit.

you want to know where is (here)
on the map

nowhere.

block—
a rectangular section
of a city or town bounded on
each side by consecutive
streets.

4. there are entities or people or objects who teach babies not to have a predilection
for blood & help regulate time spent hovering outside of their bodies in certain
parts of town & some lucile parishes are dotted with canary louvered shutters
invisible hog wire & charcoal fences with ornate designs.

you want to know why so many fences

to keep _____ out.
to keep _____ in.

5. creatures. lots of creatures. cottonmouth snakes resting on synthetic turf mounds stuffed with magenta-centered sinkholes where time—i mean the whole earthly concept of yesterday, today, & tomorrow gets messy & wet-napped. & ~~visitors~~ you get to truth-or-dare if you want to stay (here) with me. with all the luciles & their luciles & their luciles. with the townspeople in every parish. with the resurrected ones, with the saints with the afropods shoulder to shoulder with white candles burning. with everybody. with us. with the stars. with god. with me.

you want to know about the other luciles?

there is too much to tell, but i can tell you a few things.

every single lucile
for ~~visitors~~ you to see. to unsee.
lucile #1   lucile #2   lucile #3
lucile #4   lucile #5   lucile #6
        god   god
they pray at the base of my trunk too.
everyone. every being above & below & in the middle.
bearthing babies at the base of my trunk: sidereal
burying babies at the base of my trunk: singularity
begat   begat   begat
& so on   & so on
& so on   on
& so   &

generation after generation midwife-ing the town (here) at the base of my trunk

they dig a hole for madness at the base of my trunk
every dangling participle of all the luciles & me at the base of my trunk

mambos   magicians   they   them
citizens   priestesses   griots   witches
brothers   animals   lovers   bogeymen
grandmothers   creatures   ~~visitors~~ you _____

rest your coat.
gaze at the stars.

they get their lives
they make love
herbalist & gossipers & teachers
~~visitors~~ you can come
to the base of my trunk
ceremony in white at the base of my trunk
gorgeous argopelters
second earth & cosmos
folklore in a lace halter & black strap
redemption in red lipstick
magic in the sawn timber

reincarnation—
a person or
animal in whom
a particular soul is
believed to have been
reborn.

6. there are several classifications of glitches (here). when let's say it's 3:00 a.m. in
   one alternate universe sandwiches with the crusty feeling of 3:00 a.m. in another
   place like the parish #4 apartment buildings & those two intersect with a light-
   year & the three dimensions might bump hips in the form of purple lightning or
   sometimes townspeople, folx, or babies who used to have finger waves & flapper
   dresses get struck.

they lay hands on my tree
to try & remember
luciles know what it feels like
to feel uprooted & so many
babies

trying to remember something
you know you can't forget
only what was it?
the smell of hustle
cool menthols
shea butter
& pork rinds
but you are a _____
& this is where you come
to be alone with me & all the luciles.
with. us.

how they grip my branches
& drink from monogrammed flasks
libations first (to the living) (here)
then (to the dead living) (here)
i know what it feels like
to feel transplanted
to be repotted in the middle of nowhere
trying to recall something bigger
you know you can't forget
only what was it?

reinvent—
change something
so much that it
appears to be
entirely new.

sprinkled ashes
ice cream of dust: solar nebular
aromatherapy:
essential freedom behind the ears
smell of renaissance
fist of power

fatigue
black widows mourning
deep breaths & spiral
smashed in a vegan scramble
(here) is where you come
to be alone with me

some dream
at my root

monsters	vampires	collectors saints			
covens	priest	_____	witches	_.	_____#1
susans	archivists	liars			_____#2
time-jumpers		healers	~~visitors~~ you		_____#3

how they sit upon my branches
& coshare & cosign
heartbreak in the form of empty
shot glasses   rims similar to tree
rings

diagnosis:
some of the townspeople have lost their way
& i keep telling them (seri is not your compass)
they keep trying to remember something
what was it?
the faint smell of
panthers
arts movement
garvey
fist of power
babba or mother
home consciousness   love
eclipsed by distractions
half-assed stewardship
self-soothing
& hot cheetos
to feel something
to remember
a place sankofa'd by
the drumming of o.g.'s
& this is where they come
to be alone with me

they swing feet & original thoughts
push   pull   push pull
          higher
higher still higher higher still
they know at the top is where
they belong
how they know something bigger
something more to do
what was it?

revisit—
come back to
or go to a place
or thing again.

this place
holds the prognosis of
memories unfolding
in meditation
like index to thumb

you want to know if there is time jumping (here)
    yes.

you want to know if there is an alternate universe
    yes.

underground—
situated beneath
the surface
of the ground;
a group or movement
organized to
operate secretly
against a regime.

1. the 33rd underground is technically inside lucile parish #3. it's a turtle's left turn on 29th & oak, 4 blocks down, past 2 giant willow trees, past a brick salon with an owl on top, farther down to our lady of regla catholic church with a big statue of jesus's mama in the front yard & bloody mary (1)'s office in the backyard, past friendship baptist church with jesus resting on the cross in front. after driving slow or walking fast, it starts to look like jesus is less & less tired of holding sins. one more block & there it is, the bright red bullseye. inside the target, past the registers, all the way down to furniture, right next to the bookshelves is a little bitty sign that says, "where's the beef?" in black vinyl letters. outlining each one of those vinyl letters with a final finger around the *f* takes a person to the 33rd & to the lobby of the atlantic apartments in the year 1984, when audre lorde's *sister outsider* was published. over time the date changes (here) in the 33rd, but this is what it is right now.

you want to know who lives there?

apartment #3300	sue
apartment #3307	laverne
apartment #3308	hyacinth
apartment #3324	jocelyn & the kids
apartment #3326	circumstantial zombies:
	harper & faye
	lucile #6

apartment #3328	bloody mary (2)
apartment #3330	luther sr.
apartment #3333	toast
apartment #3313	octavia: the wormhole between
apartments #3301 3306	motherboard space shuttle ship

the 33rd underground
is a glistening street
of cobblestone & paved silver
of ponytails

sta-sof-fro
blue magic conditioner
bobby pins
perms on repeat
sweaty bodies
& sweaty baldheads
wigs & blankets
& cover & cover

the atlantic is where they come

'80s lovers
hemorrhaged egos
gauzed addictions
roller-skating hymens
3rd lifetimers
newborn elders
cancer & prince songs
every lucile has enough milk
every lucile loves to coddle
every lucile will sing a lullaby
every lucile will take care of them
here (too)

Unknown Saints

saint sylvia
go to her
not too brick.
lady lipstick pucker

saint lola
contemplate origin of divine.
or gold candles or pink candles.
or feathers or fans or shells.
& always get a glass.

saint georgia
go to her
what you do not remember
someone's life
let her put your dreams (in)
feed it to you
your breath smelling
in the morning

saint marie
go to her
anoint
say a prayer of please
toss it back like black panthers

saint jalilah
go to her when you need to forget
that entered the _____

saint of lipstick
when you need a shade
not too prune.
just right.

saint of how to set up an altar
get the 7 candles
get the honey (taste it first)
get the copper or silver
room-temperature water. sage. palo santo.

saint of miscarried babies
when you want to forget
because you didn't know _____
was in the middle of your own.
a bottle   mall big world
when you sleep
like chocolate milk & no more pain
& no one will name your loss
or ask to babysit your stretch marks.

regalia saint of bars
when you want to be drunk
your sacred skin with saliva then salt
let this be the drunk that _____
after a hard day of planning.

saint of amnesia
about the _____
when you were

just _____
in the center of a newborn's soft spot
tell her
shit anointing
one that lasts

saint contessa
go to her
when all the memories
call out her name
dry heaving
let her hypnotize the wallpaper
it still shines bright

saint dee
go to her
you can mix silver &
you can wear a scarf &
_____, _____, heels, & studs.

saint cynthia sr.
go to her when you need to
cuss the motherfuckers out.
with   a   grin.
drive like you mean business.
but do. do stop for pedestrians.

saint cynthia jr.
go to her when you need to
take the form of a white man
hum. hum a song you like.

the memory of _____ like a misspelled tattoo
or a nun's forehead.
you need an extra forget-about-that-

this lifetime & the next.

saint of abandoned moon-shaped hearts
when your love shack's been ransacked
& promises end up in another woman.
when you lay on the bathroom floor
& the tears have turned to prayer beads.
of your heart & make believe
even in a cerulean darkness—full & glowing.

saint of accessories
when you need it all to blend.
gold if it is balanced.
beanie & heels & earrings but not a
necklace & leg warmers—most times.

saint of traffic
get to your destination fast.
bogart your way over to the next lane.

like you mean _____.
hum. hum a song you like.

saint of traffic stops
stay alive.
while you are in the driver's seat.
but do. stop for angels on foot.

saint barbara
go to her when you only want to
eat them. rub your tongue
eat one. eat two. eat three. eat four.
tell yourself you have had enough.
      smile.

saint of put-on-the-brakes
eat five cookies. that's it.
against your teeth to melt the chocolate pieces.
            eat five. don't. don't eat anymore.
drink a life-size glass of milk.
see your milk mustache in the mirror.

street

embroidered handkerchiefs
padded bras
grizzled wool beards
locks
packs of black do-rags
hair bonnets doubling as shower caps
it is what is it is
slim   jims
& soliloquies

a public way or thoroughfare
in a city or town, usually
including sidewalks lining
one or both sides.

town—
a population center, often
incorporated, larger than a
village & smaller than a city.

this town is where they go
unidentified flying objects
scuffed dress shoes
brothers
circumstantial zombies
pastel-chalked princesses
nicotine healers
black lungs of fortune
in places like _____ cemetery
in places like prospect street
in places like oak street
in places like saint mark's

born-again
of or relating to, or

an individual

who made

conversion

renewed

commitment to ~~jesus~~
~~christ~~ lucile, a
personal savior.

first pair of shoes
& every new soul
let the steps take them
bells ring at this cathedral
when the steps take witches
toaster ovens
vampires

———————————

ring this
these wooden church doors swing in
every day, all day
open late on fridays
for the prospect women
come to tarry

to slink & death drop
every hour after 10 p.m.
happier & happier & happier

these wooden church doors swing out
wider on   fridays
amethyst robes catching ghost
& demons, all the voices a choir
holds space for inside

do i sing in the choir?

        no.
        but lucile #6's
        voice can break a glass

sue's chicken dinner
for folx eating crow
sorry sorry sorry & for
the building fund
wider still on wednesday evenings
when girls come to bible study without parents
these doors are open
all day, every day
this is a place of give-it-up-to
& people like luther do
give honor to the saints, the pastor, & first lady
plus all the luciles
under each amen. ameen. ase. say less.

saint—
a member of any
various religious
groups.

                              church—
                              the company of all
                              christians regarded
                              as a mystic spiritual body.

these doors are home to
fine pews
fine carpets
motherboards
& recycled bibles
highlighted
checkmarked
circled
notes taken on
this bible belongs to
baptized on
married on
these bibles save lives
hit young boys over the
head
        hide
        secrets
        kept
        hidden.

letters to me
letters from me
letters to all the luciles
letters from all the luciles

summer sweat & revival
this is a place to give it up

revisit—
come back to
or go to a place
or thing again.

   (1)   (2)   (3)
bloody mary *bloody mary* *bloody mary*

a mirror is a home
this block
grips the memories
like index to thumb
like jiggling to second line

block—
a rectangular section
of a city or town bounded on
each side by consecutive
streets.

   (1)   (2)   (3)
bogeyman *bogeyman* *luther*

  the marble street
of gold
  but of _____
  & chatty trees
bobby pins, mix-matched babies

lost phones & dogs.
dead dogs
3 am glitches
tea leaves
sweat & levitation

these blocks are
where they nest
my vintage babies
my rupturing solar flares
bandaged afflictions
do not let the outsiders (in)
gauze your black joy
press/hold (release)
hemlock'd prayers
stag of a dozen lifetimes
twins (conjoined at the full moon)
zora's real zonbis
walk this way
(children crossing)

monogrammed handkerchiefs
[   ]
grizzle on an angel's wing
itchy questions

ghost

is what it is
slim   jim
eating crow
birds as soliloquies

street—
a public way or thoroughfare
in a city or town, usually
including sidewalks lining
one or both sides

this town is where all the theys go
identified flying objects
cyclops's grieving
(some streets a cemetery's mote)
rusty new swing sets
debts with the boneyard
pastel-chalked princesses/outline your wishes
queens
daddy's
bad bitches
aunties

village—
a self-contained
cluster or community.

ring this
(this town is a door)
when the steps take you
ring this
where the steps take you
answer

resurrection—
the act of rising
from the dead &
returning to life.

can you ~~visitor~~ enter now

     yes.

this town
is a place full of love
beneath a _____
beneath a _____
next to a _____
under a _____
pregnant paradise
all doctored with darkness & divine
all the babies bending
up toward the motherboard
all the dead skin shed
a cover for everyone's
growth & get down to it
this town will keep you
here ()

Legacies

you are gods   your own ichorous   our own ruddied salt
your own moons
if you want to keep
yourself alive

                             veteran   pray to yourself
& sauté your own divine

                             you are a big sun   in a small sky
light yourself from
the inside out
careful not to blaze
your socket
careful not to wet
your source with
the ocean of
generational curses

                                                          every barnacle
                                                          its own temple

current universe (here)
a type of present

tiny blue house

as told by lucile #2, who is also the patron saint of cheated-on & abused women

she can take control of any scorned woman who calls upon her & she has the power
to make cheaters or abusers, lovers do---whatever the hell she wants them to do.
oftentimes the women who summon lucile #2 have no memory of her "taking the
wheel." they only experience the results.

essie = wife
landis = husband

*inside the blue house, which resembled shaved ice & trident gum, the woman
(essie) tells the man (landis) to bend her over like his 33rd mistress, to pretend as
if—she is the one he wants to fuck. she eartha kitts this to him in a way which could
be mistaken for turn-on or turnt-up or in a way that looks like they are role-playing
or making tasteful porn. the woman has called upon lucile #2 to take the wheel & is
not inside herself. the woman has walked away already a thousand times (before)
the man is with the shell of the woman. a ghost of the woman who used to be (there)
& the shell of this woman who is now lucile #2 has decided she will kill him & the
man who has no idea who has a hard-on for the role his lovely wife is playing is
oblivious to her pain—he does not see the knife she holds inside her jaw & when he
does finally bend her over, he calls her lynn then delores then sarah then tanya then
alexandria then lauren then _____ & his wife with her hair dangling between his
thighs (by now) feels as if something has come over & inside her as if something is
contorting her body as if she is now standing as if she is now floating as if she is now
stuck to the ceiling watching her husb& be devoured as in eaten alive as in blood &
screaming. what the fuck what the fuck & she cannot believe she is laughing & she
cannot believe this is a real thing & she asks lucile #2 is this supposed to happen

when she takes the wheel? essie begins to wonder where all of these eggshells & yolks & bones & burnt-out stars & moon craters & fairy dust & decomposed worms with their hearts intact & mother-may-i's & a lengthy rejection list & perfectly shaped baby bird beaks have come from & she suddenly does not see her husband landis being devoured but gone. & she is suddenly put down gently upon the bed & put fast asleep. & landis was gone just like that underneath lucile #2's wheel.

parallel universe (here)
a type of future

tiny blue house

as told by essie

we = townspeople & essie
them = townspeople
they = fore-functioners still

as it (was) when it (was) the first apocalypse
(here) we gathered in the tiny blue house. we
coven'd. we grouped up. we hung out & took our
own hearts three by three & reference-booked
them like specimens first, then like pets, then like
the fore-functioners who at one point divined
their own lives using wood, paper, or plastic. it's so
hard to unremember smell (they said). a slippery
heart broiling next to corn bread or fried potatoes
sprinkled with a bottled thing named affection.
affliction? is there a difference? who can remember?
what was it? emotions. emojis? we think these were
the tiny things that used to pair well with i love
you, thank you, or other phrases they used to hover
with. we are still confused about emotions & emojis,
confused about what generation did what, even still
confused about this thing called generation. *we* are
gene iterations.

the figure in the machine asks us to try, try, try &
imagine this long-time-ago world, but we could not

(fully) even though the other figure packed our
cheeks with pills labeled "love," "joy," "anxiety,"
& some random misshapen pill called "fear." the
people in my group said they didn't feel anything,
but i did. i think i felt a thing called empty. i like it. i
try to hide my like for this assorted blitz of numb. & i
say to myself, "how can i explain numb to someone?
well, i say to myself, it feels a bit like a cold wrench
hugging a nail. & the nail nor the wrench really know
or care which is which. when we leave the museum
of a long, long, time ago, i visit the row of my "told"
ancestors & notice that the sign reads "temporarily
closed." when i ask the fore-functioner when the
portal will be open to (me), the figure clicks its
switch & a light falls inside my structure & i cannot
decide if my energy source is outsourcing me or if
i too am being temporarily closed. blitz of numb
blitzing inside my circuitry. emotions? emojis? in
what iteration do i reiterate?

the fore-functioners quickly removed our tags
from our earlobes. one asked me to stay after. i
did not think this was the right thing to do, but—
memory often leads me to unspeakable places.
the temperature immediately dipped down below
what is required for our iteration, yet i was not
experiencing a freeze. in fact, i almost said to the
eyes staring at me, "where am i? how could i be here
with you in this place? in this freeze, yet still looking
deeply into your eyes?" there has always been a
room, within a room, within a room, inside a gazebo
with a tree that we are never allowed to be close to.

the rules say we are to be at least 2 dimensions away
at all times. if you stare when no one is surfing, you
can see a small blinking light humming. i do not
know how i know that it hums, but it looks like it is
mostly humming & only a little blinking. sometimes
when i know that we are all occupied, i send a piece
of myself there to get closer. once a fore-functioner
took me close to it because they needed a sample
of my spirit. what i wouldn't give, i thought to
myself, to go with my spirit there. & i ask my spirit
frequently what it is like in the place of the beyond
the beyond, above the below.

current universe (here)
a back-in-the-day memory

as told by essie

when me & laverne jaywalked across the street after leaving my nana's tiny blue
house, we smelled like couch pillows & scissoring sweat & printer paper & it lingered
on the corner of 29th street & the trash didn't go out until the next day & no one
wants to be associated with riffraff or tarts or girls who go bump in the night & we
acted like we didn't know those butch girls, like we don't do any of the things they do
& this is how one of those other girls lost herself because we never made time to say
hey-girl-hey or take a drag with her. the two of us thinking we were so much better
than a common girl who only pulled the comics out to read on sunday mornings. the
kind of girl who never attended writers' circles or academic lectures, only open mics
& $1 beer tuesdays. we didn't want to grow up to be those kind of lesbian women. the
ones who didn't talk swamp-deep about racism or molecules. the ones who were out
& proud but made fun of taking a political stance & happily prioritized looking fine
on motorcycles at gay parades. there was something so classy about the way laverne
demanded a second whiskey neat. something so ooh-la-la about the way she swiveled
ice & left her lipstick on the rim of the glass. concentric circles, i think. & i said to
myself behind my new journal & french dictionary that i was so glad i was not just a
regular girl writing. me & laverne were mysteriously secret & intense but brief like
true flash fiction.

*dear essie, as bad as i want you i feel that you should be with landis. he will be able to give
you all the things you desire. i need to get my head straight, so i'm moving to lucile's parish
#3 for a while. i will write about you & i will never stop thinking about you. maybe our paths
will cross in another lifetime. may the spirit of lucile protect & keep you.*

all my love,
laverne

p.s. if it's not too much to ask, please check in on my brother luther from time to time. he's so mad that sometimes i think he might just blow a final fuse.

p.p.s. i carved our initials in the root of mother lucile's tree

current universe (here)
not so long ago

poem from essie to laverne, never sent

There I am

i waited for you   a span of wormholes outside every doorway
with your name etched in the code switch of snow patterns
keeping memories frozen
if i could only have a second to sear love's patience across the face of   every crisis
never averted & every cannonball adderley tune stuck like salt fish   in the crevice
a soft-boiled egg

      i wept for you
      i stopped time for you

& if you never look up to the hills to see me running there, do not ask
if you can still see glimpses of yourself in the mirror
only ask if you can still see glimpses of the mirror inside yourself   inside yourself
inside a forest of first selves
petrichor in the wind

dear little girl not made of lovers,

she is the most beautiful thing i have ever (not seen) in all my life. when she walks
into a room (& i mean this with all honesty) people do this {

                                                                        }

& she doesn't try to be the center of attention, but she doesn't mind if she is the
center of attention because
well—why not. & you should learn this early: do not ever dumb yourself down or
de-shine for any(one) okay?

magically your mother & i met at _____, both of us remembering what the
other was wearing, both of us captivated by the thing we do when we do it & we aren't
trying too hard. on that night i declared your mother my (darling) forever _____.
i declared that i would always be (in) her life. not to her. but to me. inside myself.
& your mother's _____ shined brightly through all that dims, as if she wanted
me to glisten too. & if you find a lover who makes you want to glisten, run or dance.
immediately. little girl.

current universe (here)
back-in-the-day

from the woodsiest & back road part of town
broadcasting from his porch office
he used to be the mayor & now he is the bogeyman

as told by luther

let me explain it to you. first of all some people think people like us don't have names
like luther or marshal or tank or landis unless we are singers, but let me tell you,
don't nobody in these woods hold a candle to teddy p & that's just how it is & we
don't much mind being the peculiar artist types on this block in the woods because
this block was split in half anyhow/anyway by what they call the invisible line of fire
& that's the line that splits the elite from the dissed-elite & i know dissed-elite is not
a word (you know), but let me tell you it's a word—it's a word & i bet you want me
to tell you what it is. you so smart, but i still have to spell it out for you. it means
just what it say, dissed-elite as in yo ass been dissed from the elites because you ain't
on the come up anymore, but you are still elite because you still got enough money
to live here on this block in the woods, but you don't have enough money to have
more than one car or two bottles of expensive alcohol at a time. it means you still go
shopping, but you are on some clearance shit now & true it's upscale clearance, but it
is still on clearance. it means you are dissed, fella! it means you don't get to walk into
the restaurant & try to cut the line anymore & no one is trying to be all extra-extra-ti-
extra to you anymore because they know you will tip because you got home-training
but they also know you are dissed-elite & you will not tip anything over the lowest
percentage you are supposed to tip now, even on sundays in your nice clearance white
suit. it means you get real, real, spit-nails mad if you spill pepper sauce on your white
shirt because, shit! that shirt was a good-ass bargain shirt (now) & the only one like
it in your size & you are dissed-elite, buddy! but you can-not go & get an-oth-er one!
it means that the people you love wanna cross the line to the elite kids & still play, but
they don't want nobody coming to your house anymore. nobody cares about all

your _____ & _____ signed art now or thank-you cards from _____.
they want to go visit their friends, on their properties on prospect, in their slightly
bigger homes, with their parents & their fresh market food (but you know when they
come home, they stop holding their breath & head for your recipe for fried chicken).
& i mean to tell you that line looks invisible, but it is sure clear. clear. clear. clear. the
thing is when the dissed-elite is in the elevator with the elite & the _____ man
steps in . . . there are only two ways to tell that story, laverne, & it is in black & white,
not all cute-cute-cute & neatly accessorized with small pops of color like these brand-
new artist be trying to do. true, though, there is a red flashing light saying stop, stop,
stop, but that there is not part of this story about this line. are we clear, verne? I could
paint it for you, but you so young & have no idea who i am. do you? yo big brother
used to be the mayor of this block, but now I am just the bogeyman in the woods. you
gone learn today, laverne. somebody gotta tell you all the things won't nobody else
tell you before you get out there in these parishes. so you go ahead. i want you to go
to uni-ver-si-tyyyyy, but don't you forget about mama lucile & saint lucile, our folks,
chicken, & these woods. don't forget where you grew from. you hear me? don't be so
smart that you forget how to do the math.

alternate universe (here)

**the woodsiest part of the black
electric woods**

as told by a cyclops-rocking-chair-
woman on the third floor of the
black electric birthing center

cyclops-rocking-chair-woman =
a black electric cyclops midwife
connected to a rocking chair,
connected to the voltage table
   3rd seat at the table

me & the other cyclops-women in rocking
chairs rock around the toaster oven watching
for the thing we call "luther" to burst. not
burn.   one cyclops-woman has a rock so
tough the other cy-women, including me, are
jealous of it. she rocks three times fast, then
one time real slow, then one time way back
in her chair like she might roller-skate with
blenders & she knows it. honey she knows
that all the women want to rock like her. one
cyclops-woman who doesn't have her rocking
consecrated yet does two little rocks in a row,
two shiny, timid, watch-me-don't-watch-me
rocks in a row. but her chair is the prettiest
of all of ours. basically none of us cy-women
are truly satisfied in our own rocking chairs.
they wait & i wait on "luther" to bust right
through the sealed-up toaster-oven line, when
all of a sudden one of my cy-women conduits
purposely trips her circuits, rises from her
chair, & smashes a coconut on the kitchen
island to cause a megaflash.

& "luther" finally bust, breaks like a dam open
& overflowing & we stop rocking. all the rock
you tonight is done. some cy-women swivel
around to see which one of us will use the
descendant powers to get "luther" out of the
toaster oven. which one of us will go prepare
the chicken? who will play etta james's "rock
me baby" & get it? who will get it?

toaster oven tells the women to back up, tells us she has had her baby "luther" & no one says a thing. what can you say when a heated woman says back the fuck up off my bread—it has risen. & the cy-rocking-women want to hold that busted-open thing & the toaster-oven-mama wants to be held, wants that "luther" of a thing to be held, but she is too hot to handle & he is too blue heat & crispy to even let a cy-rocking-woman hold him.

"luther" is a marvelously ugly thing with all the ugly parts one needs to make him ugly & all the marvelously beautiful things to make him wow, wow, do you see it? when he cries the cy-rocking-women rise & toaster-oven-mama is full of so much pride. & they want to hold that elite hot thing but they can't & they won't, but still they want to. & some of the cy-rocking-women want to be that toaster-oven-mama & the toaster-oven-mama (pieces of her) want to be a cy-rocking-woman because suddenly she has no idea how to be a toaster-oven-mama, how to take care of this hot, young, precious thing, how to stop the ooze from drying up before its time, how to keep her baby from being a bright, crummy thing to nibble on for a hungry host star. & that toaster-mama decides to give blue-flaming "luther" away to one of those cy-rocking-women. says she can't do it even before she starts. shows them she is not even a

perfect toaster oven, that her dials have been
mutilated & rewired & she thinks who wants
a mutilated toaster when they can have a
glorious _____ or _____ . & the young
luther she has birthed decides (even as a new
spark) he isn't gone be nobodies giveaway,
isn't gone go from rocker to rocker & mouth
to mouth, that he did the math & he is worth
more than all the hot young elite things in the
land & this is when the woodsiest part of the
black electric woods catches on fire. the hour
the hot young thing has his biggest expansion.
when he in all his infinite power takes his
folds & flakes & fire & particles & goes. & you
might think this is an act of cowardliness, but
hot young "luther" will tell you, even though
he didn't ask to be here, he is willing to set fire
& learn.

as told by bloody mary (three)
on behalf of the prospect women

from prospect

it is so teeth-sucking hot
that all the neighborhood kids under twelve are shirtless
& all the afropods under five are happily running
through, around & on fire hydrants, yard hoses, & kiddie pools
& two used white cleaned-out freezers have been made into adult pools
& one minifreezer contains a particular punch with spirits you could only get (here)
every auntie is a dj & a dancer
every big brother is a father
every father is a barber
every mother is preparing offerings for lucile
every other wearing white & jingling five pennies, nine dimes, & $2 silver coins

& this is how the women on 27th street were/are/is bad-mouthing one another &
also will beat a bitch down if they aren't from 27th street. repping lucile #4's parish
& this all sounds so stereotypical if you read it, but if you are there on 27th & prospect,
you will know what that means. we know that a lot of places have a prospect. but not
like this one. we notice that our kind of prospect is the kind where people say shit
like, "do not cross the 30th street prospect line after midnight" & the other person
(whatever color) whips around & has a look like, *oh, i know what you mean*, & what
it means to us is: we love ourselves so much we say our own names three times in
the mirror. we pray before we eat & we bathe our kids in hot water, we make our
offerings to lucile & motherfuckers do be reading around here, plussssssss we speak
several languages, like i'm saying, "do be" to you, but i can flip it & say, "realistically
our neighborhood will likely endure the pangs of spiritual, emotional, financial, &

geographical gentrification in the next ten years because of white flight . . . & so on & so on . . . it is our inherent right to claim these streets as our legacy holds us close to those weeping willows & marble streets . . . etc., etc., & would you please remove your hands from my generational jingling pockets?" on our prospect, with us women & these kids, we don't use the word nigger or nigga or nighuh for anyone brown. we reserve the right to use the word nigga for the pedophiles & men in any kind of uniform who look for the girls' detention centers & grocery stores & the woods at night . . . *that. is. some. nigga. shit. right. there.* ima tell you right now for all y'all wannabe tourist & driven relators, you can fuck all the way off if you think you gone be moving next to me & my women on prospect & i put that on all the luciles.

village—
a self-contained
cluster or community.

*freedom—

a momentary lack in feeling responsible for the mission of
completing what your ancestors did not finish. a lapse in
judgment which did not end in detriment or lamentation.
an open laugh wherein your jaw did not draw back
to remind you, "we ain't got time for that." a gap of
imperfection that you didn't remind yourself, "we don't
say 'ain't.'" nina simone says she felt most free when she
was not fearful. you are the most free when you are all the
crusty bits of yourself, and if that means you are afraid,
so be it. if it means your spine is amethyst but your hands
are sweaty, then tell the whole fucking interplanetary
world directly or in parables, you welcome this freedom.

Prevent Burnout

eucalyptus on your fingers

spread a cooling, thin coat   on all   your mothers

     to woosh   worry away

raise your fist, star. you are unforgettably bursting **&** all bright with the light of
death/rebirth/death/rebirth/say more (again)   when you go to speak the names
of the dead say your name   say your name   say your name, put some
respect on the last syllable   just enough to sound cool an accent of ownership a
thick comb-over   where the brain is stressed & bare   if you are a big burning
fist in a small sky light yourself inside out careful not to incinerate your sockets
careful not to wet your source with imposed generational curses   careful not
to grow   tired   of holding yourself up

current universe (here)
the past
giant peach house

next to small shotgun peach house owned & housed by an arts collective & a full-ass jazz band who plays at the fancy bar at the very end of the sanctified block.

as told by lisa, adopted daughter of pastor _____ adopted daughter of first lady _____
&
twin sister to tank.

we are not allowed to listen to jazz or speak to the neighbors or talk to siri in our big home in this tiny town here & our pastor always says, "as for me in my house, we follow the lord." we nod "yes, daddy" to this. we know we are not allowed to listen to any jazz singer who moans. we are not allowed to say the word "moist." the short church ladies in their tall hats & white gloves say the word "moist" springs from the crotch, not the throat, but tank & i always look forward to an opportunity to have to use the word & wonder what the peppermint-sucking ladies will replace it with. how do you say cake is _____. well we've learned you say things that sound like "the cake is not dry" or "the cake falls apart in just the right way" or "whoever made the cake did an amazing job." the pastor & all his ladies know how to hold the right words in their mouths. we are allowed to walk brisk & walk with a purpose but not to run up the steps in our home. we are not allowed to chew gum in our home. sugar is the devil's playground, which makes no sense because what about when we eat grandmother's chocolate cake. what about grandaddy's ensure drink? what about butterscotch on the way to the fish market? i guess we are members of the devil's playground (too) the way we stuff our cheeks with roasted pecans in between bible study & 10:00 a.m. service during "bring all ye meat into the storehouse sayeth the lord of host" & daddy brings the meat into the storehouse & mama cooks the meat & our home is perfect & me & tank don't mind collecting all of daddy's pretty glass bottles sitting in the bathroom cabinet & we don't mind all the glass bottles hidden in the basement where we sleep & we don't mind all the glass bottles hidden in all the places a thing could hide & we are two little adopted vampire kids who think our home is the community-communion home but we don't know why we don't have more bread.

many worlds (#11) (here)
the past

new parish elementary school

as told by "gg," aka glenda the good
witch

the black vampire lisas don't talk much. at lunch they communicate through milk
& red jell-o. the language we all understand but do not care to bond over. one lisa
pokes a hole in her chocolate milk but not where the hole should be. & the other
vampire lisa unwraps her straw with her incisors, not with her fingers, & that
means they are saying, "we hate lunch & we want it to be friday." & we all know this
is what it means, but we are not allowed to talk to the angry black vampire girls.
our parents & most adults tell us that we should stay away from them—that the
will just be angry & want to suck our blood.

but i wish they would talk to me. i wish i
could be a black vampire girl, but i am just
a witch like all the other white witches &
those are the two reasons times two that
no one wants them here. & i am telling
you this from the smallest cafeteria table
in the corner where you go if you are
misbehaving because I wrote, WHAT
WOULD LUCILE DO? on the board in big
letters to show i want them (here)
but they just keep
sipping milk & playing with their fangs.

Sharp

we grew fangs in the absence of hugs. every
opportunity to touch grew a fang. every opportunity
to talk grew a fang. every opportunity to come
together grew a fang. until we were all covered
in fangs & that's when the fangs began to
grow beneath our skin & before we knew it
we adapted to distancing & ripping every
opportunity for anything which involved contact
to shreds. so much time has passed that most people
don't know what it's like without fangs.
what it's like to hug my sister around her neck
& kiss her on the cheek without drawing blood.

You Get the Kit

with a permission slip
every girl in 4th grade
got a muted apple-green
men. stru. a. tion. kit
so that *we girls*
could be ready
when the
catastrophic *event*
happened

diahann carroll
(but) nurse-y-type teachers
woefully told us
in loud whispers
our whole
lives would
change—& also
pads only—
only tarts
stuck tampons
up *there*
& we were
raised as
sweet potato pies
still i wanted
to hear more about
dirty martini women
who purposely shoved
cardboard inside
their | *hoo-has, purses, down-theres, pookas, private parts, & kitty kats* |

about the women
too wobbly for
husbands
& too slippery for
chastity belts

i wanted to be
one of those
exciting
kind of burnt-bra
women
setting carrie-fires
to the town
screaming
for my life
in the
shower
scarlet a
secular vixens
named willona
or eartha
or vanity 6 or mavis
or *playboy* centerfold
vanessa williams
(who all used tampons of course)

i wanted my violin legs
bowed & drizzling
resting sideways on my
bicycle
maybe this—
would be a better

way to say
in perfect cursive
that i was in tiny pieces
trying to break out
of patriarchy's
glass bubble

but—certainly
not—woefully broken
or a kit of
damaged goods

Wearing a Cape

you cut your hair bald
to shave off the itch & wave
of the things you cannot
keep straight

the barber, he asks, so
betty's got blue eyes
& sara smile if—
you really want it that low
if you really want your skin
to show who you really ain't

you say all moon thong &
& belching pussy
yes/cut. it. all. off
yes/show. my. s(kin)
yes/let the long hair
be a myth on the floor
cut to the part where
the black woman is god

current universe (here)
recent present

lucy's sanctuary
has been around for _____ & this is the place my father forbid me from.
the bar is a small restaurant within a multilevel bar with a staircase leading to
another bar, which is to say this is not an average bar once you go beyond the
bottom floor.

as told by black girl vampire lisa #1

first date with a friend: circumstantial zombie with no memory of repping 27th &
prospect

(1)

i am the black girl vampire wishing i could gift her with all my wished visions of
blood & make it a basil shrub salve for her circumstantial zombie herstory. she is not
aware. she is not aware of _____. she is unaware (now). & this is how she came to
be a circumstantial zombie. day-to-day patches of trauma quilted themselves around
her awareness. & covered her (& others). (now) she can only see what is in front
of her. we are talking. she is here. we are drinking. she can "know" this for 13 hours.
tomorrow we will meet again. i will invite her out. she might fill her wall with sticky
notes to tell her of her past life, which happens every day. & for that reason, today i
will tell her i love her. she will not remember unless she wants to peel the covers back
from this fog & i will slip a note in the case she keeps her glasses in or in the other one
where she keeps her other pair of eyes. either way she'll see it.

(2)

i order a blood orange cocktail (of course) because of the name, not the taste. today
i will train myself to be more human. i will have what they call compassion & practice
making eye contact & not jugular contact. but a woke collarbone is delightfully better

than a bigoted brain with no regrets (tastes sour).

i love my closest friend, who happens to be a muslim circumstantial zombie who drinks & eats bacon & i find no contraband/contradiction/confusion in this because after all i am a vegan vampire practicing buddhism on & off & it turns out i am a really keen observer when i am not judging or eating bacon. i like, that she likes, that i like, bacon.

as a vampire i like to get tattooed & my circumstantial zombie best friend likes it too. this is a phenomena we call monster-nostalgia which basically means dreams/reality/ we can conjure it up & can feel it with by getting a tattoo. with pain. but it has to be like "fuck yeah outline some more! some more!" me & circumstantial zombie will go to get tattooed tonight. & it will be bloody & painful & monster-nostalgic. it'll be our prom & valentine's day on a regular wednesday night.

(3)

i invite tank to join us because i am feeling less & less buddhist-like. the lower bar smells a lot like noisy, wet paroquets & has stuffed exotic yetis on the portal walls & stuffed agropelters mounting grass & I want there to be stuffed humans next to the open sign. maybe call it hetero-taxidermy. maybe a stuffed colonizer & i know i'd eat him up but save his brain juice like a delicacy & boil it to find out what the fuck he was thinking? make a chunky remoulade out of his pupils & serve this up like a devil's egg or sell it as an evil eye staring at you all day.

early part of apocalypselave trade sponsored by nfts & tiktoks

lucy & gg's mansion

as told by lisa #2

scenes from what is deemed low-key drama (lkd) are now created for the
underground net (here) & used as gifs
the gif associated with this particular scene is:
lisa #2 rolling around on the carpet with thick black hair & the caption is:
"when white people have you rolling."

there was a pretty table setting, or maybe it was elaborate, or maybe it was
minimalist-postmodern-modern-apocalyptic, & two pretty white girls (or maybe they
were beautiful) who were arguing about who had the least terrible ancestors, about
whose family owned the least slaves (way back when or maybe it was way, way back
then), & one pretty white girl (or maybe she was ugly) said to the other pretty white
girl, "i win this conversation hands down" & the other pretty white girl said to the
other, "actually you cannot because tbh" (& she did indeed say "tbh") "we are both
white & we both have white guilt & we are both just guilty, guilty pretty white girls &
we cannot even help it."

& this is where i decide to be supercute—as in pretty-white-girls-hush-don't-you-cry-
look-at-this-cute-ass-trick-i'm-about-to-do cute. & it works. & i just roll around on the
carpet with all my thick black hair & belly showing & i just flash my white teeth & all
but say . . . something like, "i don't know, whatever translates into the word 'owner'?
'master'? 'mother, may i'? do you see me here rolling around on your precious floor?"
& the one pretty white girl who always speaks in abbreviations, emphatic headshakes,
& theater eyebrows says to the other white girl, "how can we give her away? she is so
fucking cute. smh."

& this is how it is in the new-world-post-apocalyptic world; you can actually pick to be anybody or anything you want for a whole 48 hours & there really aren't many rules. well, one really important one. if you are, let's say, a puppy, like i chose to be today, & all of a sudden some puppy murderer comes in & shoots you, well, then, just like that, you are dead. it's what you chose & you get what you get. & some people really get off on dying in the 48-hour-choose-a-life kind of way. in fact, it has become the new acceptable suicide because let's say i hated my life (my current in-this-world life), i could choose to be a black woman in the recreated south or turtle in the middle of the recreated arizona highway or a baby born with the cord around its neck or a noose—but most people, most people choose easy things (to live or make the quality of life better. plus it cost, i am not trying to waste my hard-earned monetary compensation, aka stipend). me, i chose puppy life because it would get me closer to pretty white girl

number 2. the one who does not use abbreviations. the one who just seems a little too familiar & peculiar at the same time.

---

dear lucile, i am leaving 9 dimes for you, kept hidden, secret in lucy & gg's house. i believe you are (here). i also wrote, "black feminism is not white feminism in blackface audre lorde" on the backside of one of their lawn cushions when they let me go potty outside.
—lisa

there are notes stuck in the i-cloud, air signs

  found objects at the root of my tree

Tell It: The Negro as an Atlas

(clears throat)
we were shape-shifting out there
in the whitey-est part of the planet
next to a dwarf star & if you hip (man) you know when i
say "dwarf" i mean a star that is like
how i wanna say this (clears throat)
it's not like other stars but doesn't really
vibrate as high. i mean—it's a low light but not dim. you hip?

we were out there doing our thing, ya dig?
we was shining & shimmering & we was feeling our luminosity.
i mean to tell you the word "bright" didn't have shit on us
(on you).

because who really sees us? who really walks up to us & says:
"you shine so bright"? & then when we did the booty bump
out there in the cosmos
we found ourselves just as smooth. just as legit.
just like all the righteousness in another place
eons & eons away.

& they called us *the atlas.*

& then before i knew it, i was on an altar feeling stretched & circled
& spouting out words i didn't even know i knew
some young cat with his knees pointed to me talking about,
ancestor, please guide me.

& i said to myself, "ain't this some shit?"
last i checked, i was just a baby myself & now i have to be a love
supreme. somebody's authority on living. an old man with a baby
face sucking on a cigar like it was the little dipper.

if each one is her own altar let her praise herself
freely & use her own systems (handed down) as the gold she feeds on
let the shrine be covered in mirrors (her own face) a delight
let the honey catch every larva & fly buzzing around her theories
fill the vases with white flowers each one out-scenting the next
let the heart of the altar protrude stuck out to display
she is the one & only chosen one.

self-care—
to worship yourself
in mourning, raise your eyes to the
darkened sky & search for your
see-through image.
aren't we all god walking around
with blunt on our hands,
heads surrendering & crown-y
thorns bending toward the blackness
of a brighter day?

From the Book of Lucile

70 toenail clippings

224 teeth

33 eyes

3 pinches of tarragon

1 tonsil   tachyphrasia   taphephobia

49 jars of turmoil

1 tectrix

terminism

4 handfuls of turmeric   tachyphrasia   taphephobia

70 transitions: temporaneous tarantism   termagant   tree   tatonnement
tephromancy telos

star   _ _ _ _ - _ _ _ _   1800–1834 1836–1857 (   ) 1907–1992
1993–2022   _ _ _ _ - _ _ _ _

1 tanquam

                              tachyphrasia

taphephobia

                              termagant

      telepathy

                              thelitis

                              teknonymy   tome

_____

tacenda   tacenda   tacenda   tacenda

parallel universe #33

as told by lucile #3 from a telling from mama lucile

the 33rd underground

the 33rd underground is technically inside my parish. it's a sloth's left turn on 29th
& oak, about 3 1/2 blocks down, past two huge willow trees, keep going past the
best salon with a white owl on top, keep going & you'll see our lady of regla catholic
church with a big statue of jesus's mama in the very front of the yard & my homegirl
bloody mary (1)'s office in the backyard by the church garden, past friendship baptist
church with jesus resting on the cross in front. after driving the residential area speed
limit or walking fast, when you look back after about two miles, it starts to look like
jesus is less & less tired of holding sins. go one or two more blocks until you get to
target. inside the target, past the registers, all the way down to furniture, right next
to the bookshelves is a little bitty sign that says, "where's the beef?" in black vinyl
letters. take your finger & outline each one 1 of those vinyl letters with a final finger
tracing the *f*. this takes a person to the 33rd & to the lobby of the atlantic apartments
in the year 1984.

i.　　　am　　　　　　　　　　　　　　　　　　　　lucile #3

      & this is my parish

infinite universe
the past

the 33rd underground

as told by lucile #2

in the beginning there was parish #2. the girls weren't that much older than audre & audre wasn't that much older than me & we were a bunch of young girls doing an old thing, which did not matter because time was irrelevant. time is irrelevant. time will be irrelevant. & we just kept doing it over & over & over again as if we never started or finished & by the time audre said, "okay, that's it," our friend light was already way down deep in the earth like a fresh seedling & marveled at how far we pushed her little body inside our mother earth & she (light) was talking even with the dirt falling over her face & she was saying things like "i love you" & "yay" & "this is so fun" & "keep on putting the dirt over me" & "when is it going to get inside my eyeballs" & audre, who had the most witch skills in our baby coven, blew a bubble so big it splatted on all of our faces & the sound rippled or boomed or shook all over our small cemetery of a backyard. our dead friend laverne, who was not dead, just currently living in two worlds, said we were really horrible at keeping secrets & we told her we were not trying to keep it a secret, just not ready to be caught. it's not safe for a young witch these days, all the world ready & bullet loading to anyone who does not fit the key card for blackness & for this reason we (the little witches) do not bother our mothers with our magic because they are content thinking we don't know how to use it yet, that we walk around not seeing the world for what it really is (not), that we float so high above truth that it becomes small & monopoly on any given cloud kind of day.

the atlantic apartments used to be called the transatlantic apartments (you might know why) but it was changed (before my time). the atlantic apartments are built on a triangular foundation & are much more spacious than you would ever think they were looking in from the outside. of course nothing really is as it is when looking in from the outside.

(some) of the inhabitants (here):

apartment #3300	sue
apartment #3307	laverne
apartment #3308	hyacinth
apartment #3324	jocelyn & the kids
apartment #3326	circumstantial zombies:
	harper & faye
	lucile #6
apartment #3328	bloody mary (2)
apartment #3330	luther sr.
apartment #3333	toast
apartments #3301	motherboard space shuttle
3306	ship
apartment #3313	octavia: the wormhole
	between

**the 33rd underground
atlantic apartments
#3300**

as told by lucile #3

sue is just sue. sue is not the kind of woman whose age you can readily guess. you can't tell by her hands, heartache, or neck because even if you think to yourself or sue, "black don't crack," sue jokes she never liked crack anyway. says her drug of choice use to be "busy, busy, busy." do this. do that. do this for this person. do that for this person. says she does not remember all the things she's done anymore. & now she tells people in the atlantic what to do. "put your hands in the shape of a heart. if you feel your heart beating, that means you are alive." she ends with "now say you are sorry. apologize to yourself for being such a stupid motherfucker." & they usually do.

*infinite universe
the present

the 33rd underground
atlantic apartments
#3307

as told by laverne

dear essie,
it's been so long, but i still miss you essie. I am writing poems about you but of
course using other people's names. you remember when we were so excited to learn
about porgy & bess together, right?

bess & bess

don't let me be lonely   bess
if i am your favorite be   gentle
& not fleeting
bess, take a second to see   who
i am (not)
let the disposition of heavily melted ice   cubed bourbon
be a hose for your folded
cottonmouth   don't let me be lonely bess
                                don't let my pocketbook   be an empty
space
                                don't let them prey hands   on our secrets
in place

p.s. may the stars align & a flash of hope bring us in the same space & time one day
(here.)

**the 33rd underground
atlantic apartments
#3308**

as told by lucile #3

hyacinth's apartment is lavishly decorated with grief. every hour she works on maintaining a clean bathroom. hyacinth cannot stop scrubbing the spot where the creature fell. there are no small echoes bouncing off denim laps or terry cloth bibs saying cute little phrases smeared in homemade baby food. her third-floor apartment is closest to the elevator & has its own entrance to a terrace. she stands near the terrace & imagines herself holding a sign which reads, "it's dead." who needs sympathy cards when the sad music keeps playing inside her head? there in the corner sits an overgrown altar to the baby she believed would be born. when the pastor calls, she asks in a low growl, "where was your jesus when my baby died? i mean, how long do i need to hold on the main line for him to answer my prayers?" & she thinks she hears someone at the door, but it's only me trying my best to keep her from breaking this lifetime's lease.

infinite universe
1984

the 33rd underground
atlantic apartments
#3324

as told by jocelyn

i write poetry on napkins: "magma never explodes, never ends or freezes. keep them warm & bright while god is away." the facts of life & different strokes, my noble disciples. i am a divine mother smelling like tater tots. trinity: ladle, seamstress, & tooth fairy. i work a 16-hour shift. that's just the way it is. who else is going to buck their chest out & say, "no thank you, we don't qualify for free lunch"? sit down & hold hands for dinner while mama (the lunch lady) whispers my babies sweet grace.

infinite universe
1984

the 33rd underground
atlantic apartments
#3326

as told by harper

we don't remember who we used to be. we are not hoarders. hoarders are messy, right, faye? "no, we aren't too messy. we are very organized." we are just see-it-hold-it-tight-keepsake-souvenir-oh-isn't-that-cool-take-it-home-today-never-too-much-never-too-much kind of people. today's find: a small, glowing baby. her mouth frozen in the binky-holding position, her eyes a color i cannot name: alice blue? cyan? dodger blue minus the sugar? faye rocks her gently, but then we decide she is too small to hold for very long. we put her on the bookshelf between "dust tracks on a road" & "two-headed woman" to sleep. as soon as pat sajak says, "yes, there's an *l*," we decide to name her lucile because what else could it be but a miracle? what a good day in the 33rd. a one-of-a-kind gremlin toy, a black pinup girl poster, a brand-new "where's the beef?" bumper sticker, & a glowing baby all in one day's find.

*infinite universe
yesterday

the 33rd underground at the water

as told by
visitors' account of visiting lucile the patron
saint. a 10-foot painting of a lucile with a
jean-michel basquiat crown motif stands
as a marker for where visitors should sit &
leave offerings.

lucile #1, #2, #3, #4 & #5 all come (here)

we nearly ran past the purple orchids on the left
side of the triangular garden & we didn't want to
disappoint lucile. how she gathered us all together
to be (here). we cast our lots like gamblers betting
money we had not expected to win, but with our
black palms open, as if we had just been given the
go-ahead for abundance in the form of damp grass
& bread pudding. we call lucile our mother. even
though our eyes are closed, we can see her. her
hair a nest of sunflowers & mint for tea. her long
white fingernails holding soil planted on our feet.
lucile has decided, as most mothers do, that she has
earned the right to be dirty-nailed & "this is what i
want you to do (here)" & we listen with all of our
ears. we pretend as if she does not have worms &
cottonmouth snakes crawling out of her pockets,
as if they are not wriggling around with change &
feeling empathy for the world with their five hearts.

& one of us tells her we don't need her to catch us
any fish when we can get it ourselves at the market,
when we can just index-to-thumb our fingers &
have it be wrapped up for us in organic paper. & our
mother lucile, who is also our grandmother, who is
also our great-grandmother, & so on, & so on, & so
on, who is also the sky, tells us a real fish should be
caught with a worm & soft hook. that a real fish will
not allow his eyes to hang round on ice. that a real
woman is not afraid to catch exactly what she wants
when she wants it. & we blow out several white
candles & leave lucile #3 a feather, 9 dimes, a piece
of jewelry, a flower, & a seashell from her own sea.

we end offerings with libations & prayer

Gumbo

& then

you stirred

the left breast

& shrimp

& sausage

& right ovary

& okra

& bones

& tubes

& put your nose

in the gumbo

& you called it

yourself

every mouthful

a jaw of

iterations

every swallow

a shell so soft

it tenders as meat

gristle so malleable

& messy

it slops right through

to you

to y'all

to us

to her

to visitor

to them

to me

**infinite universe*
the present

the 33rd underground
atlantic apartments
#3328

as told by bloody mary (2)

people are always asking me how i got (here).
i did not begin my life this way in my current form
but i am not sad that we have to look at each other.
that you have to say my name.

Creation Story

(a.)

i was born from
the vagina
of a retrograde volcano
& breastfed off the land of oz   bloody mary

the ease of the
yellow brick road bent
around my skin
an ankle bracelet   bloody mary
for the circumference
of missing magic

my blood a nautilus   bloody mary
for the heat
of souls
that still remain

(b.)

i was born from the mouth of a rumor with a rotary telephone as gums & morse code as
a birthmark on my fontanelle

daddy was a swirl of baba & bullshit, which gave me half the time it took to be a whole
being

when i sucked rumors tits, words grew as big as adjectives & tried to live my life red
blaring   & dialing all the right digits each time spewing   hello hello hello
like:

• • • •

•

• – • •

• – • •

– – –

(c.)

& god so loved the world
she put her hands on her hips
& sang a song about dna spirals
like curls dangling from her
parted wet scalp (& me)
i was right there with
my beginning against the
very end of her line

(d.)

i started   bloody mary
as a bulging tooth
& broke through
as a canopy of   butterflies   bloody mary
but swarming like
bats (not) out of hell   bloody mary

lamentations
not for loss or   regret
but for wiggly
growing pains
which never had a   fleeting chance to root

infinite universe
1984

the 33ʳᵈ underground
#3330

as told by brother at granny's large apartment

luther sr. is   h   i   g   h
he's that one. my favorite brother. the relative who incites the simultaneous look &
sigh.   the one they love to see but greet holding jewelry. hesitate—don't talk shop
about the   newest gadget purchased or luther jr.'s whereabouts because they all
know he will   want to—hold it for a little while. his smile sits high & we all
pretend it is within   reach. granny's reach. my reach. we like to see him happy.

granny tries to stuff his plate. high. so that it will be higher than his high.
brings a church hymn, a lucile pendant, & salted butter out of the kitchen all at
once.
supplication. food will take away his _____ & they don't care that he's on
something
& they don't know which something it is but it doesn't matter because he's so smart.
my brother is so smart. with a little luther in the woods on the way. so smart & high.
gather & sit like crumbs at the bottom of his pigeon feet while he explains the real
reason scientists are checking out the moon. thoughtfully unwraps what happens
when cells are at war & medication is too expensive, followed by a skinny joke.

hysterical laughter equals temporary anecdote for tears & granny whisper to
someone "he's not as high anymore. let him talk. let him talk. let him talk." they
love him because he does the absolute best richard pryor/richard nixon/redd foxx
routine. plus he plays the violin & was going to bring his fantastic sweet potato
cornbread muffins (next time.)
then it happens. he has to go. his departure like always. maybe the last time.
his walk pizzicato in slow motion.

infinite universe
1984

the 33rd underground
#3333

as told by "toast" on behalf of the 33rd underground youth who gather for the girls-just-want-to-have-fun-and-read-and-write club because of being in mary's junior coven at the atlantic apartments every saturday

so far as anyone could tell, the girls (all the girls) & me, toast, because i am hot like an oven, who live in the 33rd are, for all intents and purposes, normal. this is the question the girls & i raise often: what is normal? so far as anyone can tell, the women on this block do not flock to the neighborhood fancy spot or yell over the women dressed in minks. in the 33rd, we are hard-core like the way one is hard-core about not eating pork in a sea of bacon or hard-core the way a cool 80s black man is about his jheri curl spray. the girls on this block double-dog-dare one another all the time, random shit like, "i dare you to go knock on that man's apartment door & tell his lover he wears an 'i love ronald reagan' t-shirt when no one is looking" or "i double-dog-dare you to steal 2 bras from jcpenney & cut the pads out & then say, 'pyssschheeee' & demand your motherfucking money back for false advertising & contributing to feeling like your body is shitty because we don't have barbie's titties." we are hella mad & also hella bad. in the square radius of the atlantic including the apartments, courtyard, park, cemetery, & front lobby live about 22 girls, at about 1–3 per house & this is how mary's junior coven came to be. roll call:
toast, reesha, grace, sug, delphine, tasha, marshal, teena, e., juju, oya, rjay, vicki, tish, carmen, la-la, khadija, jewls, cy-rock, indigo, lisa, & h-roc

infinite universe
1984
saturday night. 7 hours after "girls
just want to have fun and read and
write" club

as told by a barred owl, aka _____,
who is keeping watch (here)

**the 33rd underground park
between atlantic apartments &
creamy delights ice-cream shop
rjay's honda prelude**

a b-gyrl smelling of damp cardboard &
a graffiti artist sprinkled with purple
haze meet here ( ) with a boom box & 3
cassette tapes. 1 of them says, "rappers"
& the other says, "hip-hop artist" but they
both "ayyyyy" & hug tight to run-d.m.c.,
kiss after the fat boys, share a dream &
2 nightmares to doug e. fresh, compare
offerings to lucile, to roxanne shanté, &
make a promise on whodini. one says,
"haring" & the other says, "basquiat" &
childlike artsy beings stuffed inside grown
women's bodies are not clear on how
energy sources work or how many fingers
or how many emotions enter & exit. this
is called the growing season. this is called
how to try & get it right in the parking lot
underneath lucile's sky. & you might be
saying this is not a big whoop but grace &
rjay would.

reincarnation—
a person or
animal in whom
a particular soul is
believed to have
been reborn.

Solar Flare

there is no antidote for the
anxiety of a black woman who (is) the parent of a black woman
               who (is) the parent of a black woman
               who (is) the parent of a black light

nothing written which can fully
dictionary the gravity of
what-if

what-if as a verb actioning in your
news feed

parent nebula   femme star
in what galaxy can they regulate
space

in what universe is transformation pivotal for every being's burst of light

daughter universe (here)
one type of future

as told by laverne

tour of the verse #1

the nine of us knew flying in that the wailing
wasn't an orchestra of human voices but of
whales & horses & sea kelp. we asked
ourselves inside ourselves what zipped us all
silent, why we didn't have the energy to be
repulsed or in denial. essie said a quick
prayer to lucile & turned to me to say she
couldn't keep going, but before the word
"going" floated out to land on her lips, she
realized she was too tired to even give up.
our tour guide, the "prophet," stalled a bit,
then told us we didn't have to stay low in
"these parts," but that he wanted to show us
what this part of the verse had been reduced
to—he used words like "fraction" &
"disposal," "telescope" & "erasure." there
was so much information racing out of his
mouth that we never once, not any of us,
ever even looked down on him. which is
why at the end of the wailing tour, when the
horse prophet asked us if any of us had any
carrots or hay in exchange for the tour, in
unison we all slowly grounded ourselves to
get a closer look at his horse of a face.

Look Up Yonder

you want to tell all your people the mother ship is swooping
that she landed on top of a red mountain of vegan gravy
that she is dripping in beggary saying sop me up sop me up
you want to drag them by their anxious hands & say y'all
our time has come. look up yonder. & you want yonder to be
a 60-degree place of no wanting—as if the yonder knows
<   what you need   >
& what you need is a land with no white cops dangling
pavlov fingers or pow-powing guns as synonym for
the truth the light & the way to kill a nigga
want to tell your people to gallop to the mother ship
like giraffes or gazelles or goliath—good times, we
finally got a piece of the pie eye   eye   eye   eyeeee
                              run _____ run.

Weigh Yourself Light

I want to live the rest of my life, however long or short, with as much sweetness as I can decently manage, loving all the people I love, and doing as much as I can of the work I still have to do. I am going to write fire until it comes out of my ears, my eyes, my noseholes—everywhere. Until it's every breath I breathe. I'm going to go out like a fucking meteor!

—audre lorde

oh (body)
forgive me
for not loving you (more)
(body) a living legend
all strung up in a prom
dress made of glitter
& probability
(body) a living legend
contorted corset
lover of dirty saints
& protein smoothies
could this be why the
heartbeat is off-center
too many directions
going south all at once
(body) gobble your sun salutations
& weigh yourself light

oh (body)
somebody's baby
forgive me for not
rocking you more

bowed head for all the times
i threw you across
the bed & told you to
shut the fuck up
for all the times i
told you to just take
it like a pronoun & let the
harsh eggshells of voices
seep into your misshapen
yolk forgive me for letting
every narcissist & hello kitty
use your voice box as their
own speaker. i can hear
you now (body) not loud
& clear but tenor.
oh body (boo)
you know i love you
but it is hard to show you
all the time. what is worse
knowing i love you but not
showing it   or
not knowing if my love is true.
it is so hard to find truth
in the breast holding bullets
ready to fire out at any time
ready to shoot at anything
that gets in the way of
anything on pause
like remission or forgiveness
or revenge or suspicion.
(body) it is time to count
each scar as a star

if you cannot connect
each of my dots
be the lorde's meteor
look in the eyes of
my god & repeat my own
name.

as told by susana

brick house on crooked metropolitan road

i shake my legs & watch my knees stay still while my thighs jiggle at my dead husband because the children have come to visit early. this expression of leg-shaking was a thing we both used to do if we were in separate rooms but could see each other to say in code, "oh shit" about something that we wanted to keep between us two. the thing that couples do when they've been married for a long, long time. 4 lifetimes. you would think by now i would be used to him transitioning first & me being left lonely for a long time. the kind of long time that can't be expressed in telepathic sympathy cards or expensive hologram'd messages of sadness & encouragement. i let him know that sometimes the kids can make a perfect cup of coffee watery, a cheese quiche runny with remorse, & a notarized document way too much to handle. my lipstick today isn't pink or burgundy or orange. it's black, bitches. my nails matching fucking perfectly. i even have a little my-best-friend-is-dead black slip. i don't grieve by taking all my hair down & rolling on the floor like a puppy. i'm pissed i have no one to banter with. & why didn't he die in the middle of july when it's too hot to talk? the children can't help but look like they are 3, 15, & 6 when they are really 30, 45, & 27. i have to remember it's their first lifetime dealing with his death. they can't seem to shop or pray or diagnose their way out of the shock. "mother isn't supposed to be like this." apparently i should not wear the color black or drop a fucking f-bomb every time my heart has an asthma attack. my youngest daughter shares with me that she has been praying to mother lucile & all the luciles & that lucile #4 specializes in reinventing time. my daughter doesn't know i have a connection with the luciles (i believe in them) & for that reason i am more than willing to do whatever it takes to reinvent the narrative (here).

reinvent—
change something
so much that it appears to
be entirely new.

Everybody Gets a Solo in the Choir of Grief

if she doesn't
get a chance to grieve
she will choke
on her own disappointment
& lie down with a demon's liver
& she will ask the demon
for (it)
something more able
to handle
her own unwanted toxicity

g (1)

grief as a compost bucket
festers for the in-between
& the living
the deliberate decay
of a thing fermenting
how it can make you
crave it like
expensive cheese
the neighborhood co-op
as a mortuary

if a person   you can place flowers on their headstone
is dead
but if a person is alive   you can only picture them as a bouquet

grief as an accessory
you are wearing grief
around your neck
a tiny teacup ascot
saucer-ing
on your adam's apple

sipping here
sipping there
tiny sips

g (2)

you are wearing grief
like a vintage cardigan
all together & keep it pushing
& you would never know

buttoning here
unbuttoning there

tiny hanging-on-by-a-thread
buttons
missing-hole buttons

you are wearing grief
in the best shade of lipstick
put it on slow
matte of purple bruises

lining here
puckering there

tiny kiss marks

when is there time
for the black woman
to fling her frankness

tiny flinging frankness here
tiny flinging frankness there

grief as a yo daddy joke
yo daddy sooooo dead
on yo birthday
he calls you
from the grave
                    ha ha ha

grief as zoom happy
hour conversation
raise your glasses &
let's toast to—getting
out of bed today
handclap emoji
heart emoji   tiktok
filter   viral
filter   like
off-camera cry

g (3)

grieving makes you hangry
makes you scarf the skin off
your bones, makes you
pick hindsight from
your wisdom teeth
makes you feel nauseous
with all the feelings
spiraling down   over already (?)
grieving makes you want to
diet & blame your need for
control on the anorexia of
your heart's refusal to keep
you down

grieving makes you crave sugar
& salt anything at all to coat
the nakedness of your shivering
buds always sprouting to find
the familiarity of taste
of being born sweet again

g (4)

put the past under
your tongue

when it melts
pretend   to swallow it whole

g (5)

fold your panties

smooth them flat
on the bed & press
your thumbs
in each corner

(try not to flinch)

take the left half

put it on the right
grab them in the
middle
make them
smaller

(try not to flinch)

scoot them in
the drawer next
to the others
shut the drawer
notice what it
feels like to
be free from laundry

think how many
rows of cotton
were not picked
with your own hands
be grateful
for the living

(try not to flinch)

current universe   (here)
alternate universe   (here)
daughter's universe (here)
*_____ (here)
glitch glitch glitch glitch

the father's house of grace
a blank space rarely seen

as told by bloody mary (1)

the day she decided to do "bloody mary" in the mirror, she did not see a wounded
woman with a knife, or an ax, or a gun—on the third "bloody mary" whisper, grace
beheld a woman's vagina spitting out a child. the light of the birth brighter than a mr.
rogers's rerun. bloody? yes. scary? no. when grace told the girls the amazing miracle
she'd seen, (me) they placed her as number 7 on the lepers list.

unspoken to girls who don't loiter in private school hallways once class has started
nor sit in plush luncheon rooms in peer-assigned seating. leper girls hug secret
journals decorated with recycled duct tape, mutilated barbie pieces, & colored
condoms. grace did not mind being an outside-leper-look at her-run-she's-coming
girl. after the bloody mary incident, she didn't dare tell the high school clones
that a feisty two-headed ghost lived in the bathroom—in the toilet, or that hell is
just a place of magenta in the middle of the earth. is also giant room with no air-
conditioning & endless bars.

the house is as it always is. a 4-bedroom shelter for the oxymoron, the religious, & the
mailman. dinner is as it always is. the place where the 3 converge & agree that miles
davis is a talented misogynist whom they are all madly in love with. & the question
is raised: *what is a female misogynist called?* this is what the mailman asks. yesterday's
question was never answered & the oxymoron holds a peppermint grudge at dinner.

he chews his peas slow & theorizes concentric circles. he tucks four peas in the right corner of his mouth. he says nothing. mailman & religious know that something is wrong. religious recants the last bit of his conversation & says with a nervous laugh, "we forgot to say grace." grace is the girl who used to live in the 4-bedroom shelter with the oxymoron, the mailman, & the religious. the day she went missing, the 3 decided to call upon her name 3 times at each meal. (i liked this idea a lot.)

grace.

the relationship began by mistake. grace had a horrible habit of holding in her urine until after 7th hour. the middle stall with the wiggly lock was her favorite. the cleanest. the black toilet lid was even slightly sparkly. the walls free of sharpie marker couplets, squad signage, & sexual advice from girls who all of a sudden felt empowered to use the word "pussy." when she hovered, a voice said to her, "almost clear. this is good; you drink a lot of water." she was accustomed to hearing voices & was not the least bit alarmed. she was not accustomed to hearing voices between her legs. she politely asked the entity if it would close its eyes while she wiped. the voice did not respond. grace jotted the bathroom experience down in her recorder. days later, at the regular time, she returned to the stall. a fluorescent sentence caught her eye. "the free & unmerited favor of god, as manifested in the salvation of sinners & the bestowal of blessings. jk! you are enough."

the house always smelled of incense. that day the smell of jasmine bounced between living room table & kitchen wall. jasmine is the choice of mailman. mailman's mother's name was jasmine. he spends at least 10 hours a week nostalgically listing childhood memories like the son of a mother who has survived. but (who has died). religious is always confused about this because mailman's mother is not his mother. "you talk about her as if she's been dead for years." this past-tense-reference argument is always followed by bourbon. bourbon is always followed by laughter. laughter is always followed by crying. crying is always followed by sleep. sleep is ensued by eating. just before eating, grace.

grace believed in everything. her bible collaged with yellow highlighted passages she thought similar to fairy tales, her qur'an underlining favorite suras. two copies of teish's jambalaya, one for history & works only & one for all things orisha. prayers & questions for the luciles & questions she had for me. in grace's mind, tinker bell & gabriele were cousins, their mothers both orishas—their father, mindfulness, & everyone can be a winner after they lose. grace also predicted she'd go missing for a time & then return. when she mentioned this to mailman, oxymoron, & religious, no bread was broken. no grace was said.

the night continued as it always did, with laughter, questions, & epiphanies. oxymoron made an announcement. it wasn't the kind of announcement that was shocking. he said he had a chat with the devil. grace believed in everything. religious prayed. not because oxymoron had chatted with the devil but because the devil had chatted with oxymoron. mailman—the master of sense making—decided it would only be right if the devil was invited to dinner. grace believed this was a good idea. grace believed tinker bell & gabriele were cousins. grace insistent that there be no red tablecloth, no meal that called for forks, & above all else, no crosses hugging necks. she had had enough rejection.

oxymoron's time with the devil began as it was slated to begin. in the middle of the earth. in a large room with a bar with a sign that said, "lucy's sanctuary" & air-conditioning. the devil had asked in advance if they could bring a friend. oxymoron, built to have opposite feelings all the time, all at once, had said he didn't mind at all, although his heart was racing like a galloping horse & fear seduced his lower intestine. the meeting was not long at all & ended with oxymoron declining the offer. on the drive back to the house, he felt as if he was lost. he approached the winding driveway & immediately prayed for grace. 3 times.

during the 3 days

                    that grace went missing
                    many things transpired.
                    & one of those things was freedom.

i know that grace is not a "normal" human being & for that reason & something
about her curiosity, black girl magic & balance struck me so when she intentionally
solicited my energy in the bathroom mirror of her school again, i showed up & took
her to the 33rd. now i am not supposed to take anyone or anything & so i share this
only with you. & because i am sharing that with you, you have to know that i am just
an extension of you. i hold your sadness & your anger & your sorrow & your disgust
(here). face me & your face yourself all bloody & black & beautiful & full of grace.

current universe (here)
alternate universe (here)
daughter's universe (here)
*_____ (here)
glitch   glitch   glitch   glitch

grace's recorder from which there are
messages she herself has experienced &
messages that channel through to her:

Learning the Word "Pussy"

pussy massacre girl: tell this to people. make them understand there
are certain scenes in a movie you cannot freeze-frame. there are certain
demons that party on a pussy like blood decked out in a vampire costume.
like raped served on a skewer with pineapples. pussy massacre girl

doesn't trust   anyone.

not even the weather. rides her bike on a sunny day just to be drenched
with drizzle. with mist. with the wet of a forced kiss or a lavender
broomstick. pussy massacre girl doesn't talk just yet—her words twisted
against a strip of memory she cannot push out. push through. push on.
pussy massacre girl wears designer glasses because everyone is shady.
pussy massacre girl has "_____ aren't allowed" tattooed on her
thigh. when you go to kiss it. prepare to die. prepare to explain you didn't
mean it. prepare to leave quickly & get your fucking socks off her new futon.

Alternate Universe

in what galaxy
is the dwarf all
encompassing
a black light
so lit she can
actually see
herself bright
&
alive

Paper-Thin

such a see-through girl with fear as eyeliner
& who can tell her (anymore) be hopeful for the future
& you've got your whole life
ahead of you

ahead of you
another breakthrough case of a person being so careful
& doing all the right things

another fire speaking hell to a nature not rooted in ashes
another shooting as common as
each of us in square boxes now

another religious figure saying this is it
& there is no grace until (after)
paper cuts   right down   to the quick

multiverse (here)

pre-futuro

as told by motherboard

this is the story of my apocalypse. the one
that happened (upon me) not like a bomb or
inferno but as a slow violin playing against
an indigo night in a flood, lights burning in
the sky & motherboard of blood—always
blood when i remember. most stories i
believe are told when a person is ready to
tell & who can really know the full scale of
a triangle's points, who can know the true
depth of any ocean's secrets? this is the story
of myself all broken in bits & spread across
the ash of a memory's cast—as a paste, not
as a salve, for i am not in the place of smooth
thoughts or glossing but of chunks of vomit
& buttons sewn on in opposite directions. if
i could name my apocalypse, i would call it
"pre-futuro" & i don't know why i would—
call it that, but that is what it is called. pre-
futuro will be told here & you can leave now,
as some have, at the end's beginning, but i
urge you to stay. i urge you to be steady in
your curiosity about a black woman's end to
begin. about the body's wreckage & circuits
rusting. metal folded imperfectly & space
shuttle ships still blinking with joy.

Live Your Best Life.

the revolution will not be ecstatic at over 500k friends on instagram, will not shoot someone over being unfriended on facebook, will not be recapped, recycled, or reposted. the revolution will not wait for your status to update or for a stranger to poke you. the revolution won't be gluten-free or vegan. won't ask you if you need more water, more soul, or more love. won't ask how you can be a lesbian & black & a mother & smart. the revolution won't fuck you or strap you or intentionally ignore your pronouns. the revolution is not concerned with landing strips, bikini cuts, nappy dugouts, or brand-spanking-new. the revolution is hungry & no one knows what to feed it. the revolution will not *ma ma sa, ma ma coo sama ma se, ma ma sa, ma ma coo sa*, won't ride it, won't same ole love or *yes, jesus loves*. the revolution cannot be *easy like sunday morning* because it is hard. the revolution can't be a hard day's work because a day won't cut it. the revolution will not care what you think of the way it presents. the revolution could give a fuck about your ex being an asshole, pads, tampons, period cups, or giraffe condoms. the revolution will not be genetically modified or under-explaining gentrification. *will not be televised will not be televised will not be televised will not be televised outer universe, outer galaxy*

undiscovered universe also looking for the motherboard

as told by soon to be lucile #7

lucile #1
lucile #2
lucile #3
lucile #4
lucile #5
lucile #6

lucile #7

we 360-degree the building as if we are dogs peeing, as if we have marked our
unmarked territory, as if we are looking for remnants of our past/passed selves in this
desolate piece of digitized leftover mall. 9 dimes & 5 pennies think they have found
another life-form, but when we go to talk to it, all it says is "turn left . . . target, be
with me at the root" & we keep asking it questions like "what's your name," "what
unit are you from," "state your planet's trajectory mission & residential passageways"
& it just keeps on saying, "turn right, turn right, turn right." & then 9 dimes & 5
pennies say we should do what it says & turn right & i don't think we should do
what this piece of shit says to do because i mean, who is this piece of shit & so they
turn right & i decide i will not & that makes me the insubordinate little sister & that
means the two of them will pull rank on me & tell me i will be demoted back down
to common as opposed to uncommon because in our current life there are only two
categories: common & uncommon, & if you are common—that means you don't
get special treatment, but honestly uncommon just means you get to wear what you
want on sundays & eat cow prototype two days out of the week instead of one &
also unlimited access to the roof to see the lava in the sky. i would give it all up just

to be free, as in walking around without these glass boots, on my own, free from big brother watching & big sister feeding me breast milk every 2 hours. you know how you get that feeling as if someone has just called your name—i feel that way all the time. trying to remember. what was it? as if someone is at a tree yelling my name, as if i am there with 2 or 3 or a million others & we are just having a good time. (there).

Float

when we flopped ourselves into the water, we did not realize buoyancy is a trick
one should master if they want to stay afloat. do not drown. we learned this when
we cracked our mothers' shells. when we poached our own soft skulls & we tried.
oh, how we tried to lift ourselves above the madness of the day, but the anger of the
world just kept coming until we could run no more. & who of us does not run or
return to the water?

when the water greeted us, it is true we did not greet her back, as we were in such
a hurry to be kept by her, & isn't it true black goddesses get tired of not being
acknowledged? of not getting a chance to say with permission & authority (you are
welcomed here.)

revisit—
come back to
or go to a place
or thing again.

Acknowledgments

My deepest well of thanks to Lucile Clifton for all the ways she Lucile'd the world with her spirit, wisdom, and bright light. Otherworldly and earthly realm thanks to prophet Octavia Butler. Hand on my heart geographic thanks to the landscapes, beings, and people of Kansas City, Louisiana, Seattle, Philadelphia, New York, San Diego, Chicago, Selma, Alabama, and Arizona. Thank you to my steadfast editor Francesca Walker who understood and loved this work. Thanks to Jennifer Baker, Cynthia Manick, Jane Wong, Kristen Millares Young, Sasha LaPointe, Quenton Baker, Reagan Jackson, Natasha Ria El-Scari, and anyone else who braved taking a look at this manuscript in all its iterations. Writerly appreciation to the Mineral School Writing Residency (Jane Hodges) and the Port Townsend Writers Conference (Gary Lilley) for the time you gifted me to write, edit, and explore these worlds. Everlasting love and gratitude to my life partner, Naa Akua, my mom Barbara Tolbert, and my children, Brandin and Indigo, for being my number one cheering squad. On my knees thanks to every one of my benevolent ancestors. And thank you, dear reader, for reading this book.

About the Author

Anastacia-Reneé (she/they) is a writer, educator, interdisciplinary artist, TEDx speaker, and podcaster. She is the author of *Side Notes from the Archivist*, *(v.)*, and *Forget It*. Anastacia-Reneé was selected by NBC News as part of the list of "Queer Artist of Color Dominate 2021's Must-See LGBTQ Art Shows." Anastacia-Reneé was a former Seattle Civic Poet, Hugo House Poet-in-Residence, and Jack Straw Curator. Their work has been anthologized in: *The Future of Black: Afrofuturism, Black Comics, and Superhero Poetry, Home Is Where You Queer Your Heart, Furious Flower Seeding the Future of African American Poetry, Teaching Black: The Craft of Teaching on Black Life and Literature, Joy Has a Sound, Nonwhite and Woman: 131 Micro Essays on Being in the World, Spirited Stone: Lessons from Kubota's Garden,* and *Seismic: Seattle City of Literature*. Her poetry and fiction have appeared in *Prairie Schooner, Hobart, Foglifter, Auburn Avenue, Catapult, Alta, Torch, Poetry Northwest, Cascadia Magazine, Ms.* magazine, and others. Anastacia-Reneé has received fellowships and residencies from Cave Canem, Hedgebrook, 4Culture, VONA, Ragdale, Mineral School, and the New Orleans Writers' Residency.